This Starfish Bay book
belongs to

....

Seed
Magic

Written by Natalie McKinnon
Illustrated by Margaret Tolland

STARFISH BAY
CHILDREN'S BOOKS

In a quiet corner of a quiet garden
lived a shy and gentle spider.
Tucked in her leaf she listened to
the sounds around her.

Drip, drip, drippety-drip
came the sound of the garden tap.

Swish, swoosh, swishety-swoosh
came the sound of leaves rustling
along the garden path.

Twit-twoo, twit-twoo
came the sound of the owl
family high in the tree.

Homely sounds surrounded Little Spider
as she lay smiling in her cozy, curly leaf.

Day after day, she listened to
the peaceful garden song.
Drip, drip, drippety-drip.
Swish, swoosh, swishety-swoosh.
Twit-twoo, twit-twoo.

But there was one sound that was not so peaceful, and it kept Little Spider awake.

Hurry, scurry, worry-worry.
Hurry, scurry, worry-worry.

Peeking out from her cozy,
curly leaf, Little Spider spied
a busy ant hurrying and
scurrying from place to place.

"5, 6, 7... I must search further."

"8, 9, 10... I must find more."

"11, 12, 13... never
enough, never enough."
All night long Anxious Ant
hurried and scurried and
worried.

"Oh, Anxious Ant, what is bothering you so?" asked Little Spider.

"Winter is coming!" exclaimed the ant. "Soon the ground will be cold and the autumn seeds will shrivel and freeze. What will I have to eat when the seeds are gone?"

And on he went, hurrying and scurrying, to collect as many seeds as he could find.

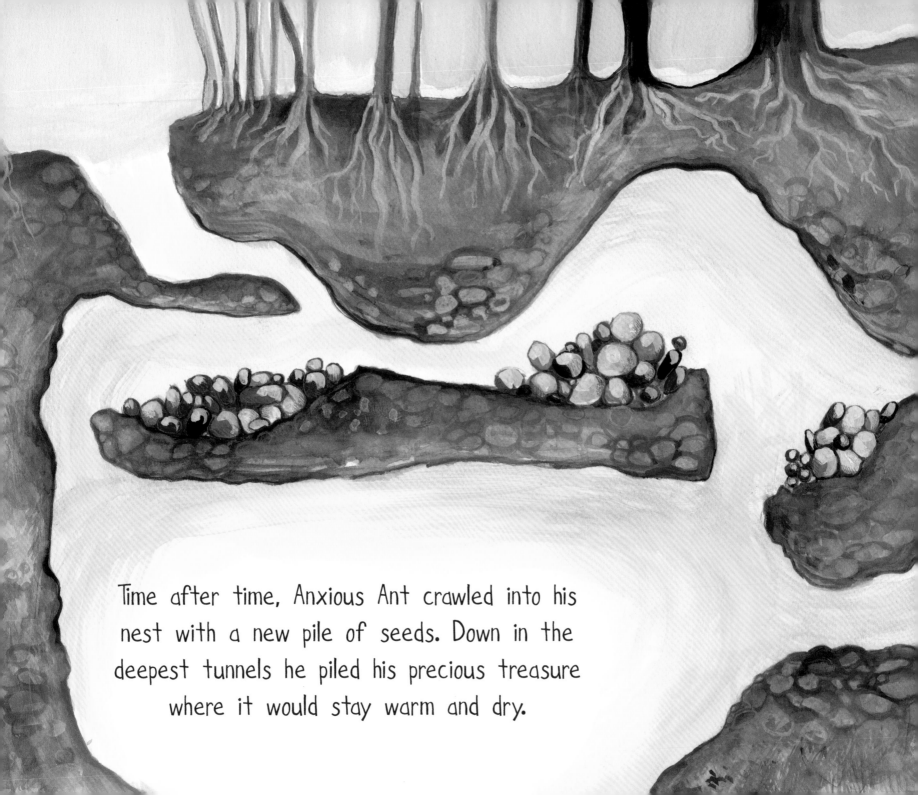

Time after time, Anxious Ant crawled into his
nest with a new pile of seeds. Down in the
deepest tunnels he piled his precious treasure
where it would stay warm and dry.

Hurry, scurry, worry-worry.
Hurry, scurry, worry-worry.

Little Spider watched in dismay as
Anxious Ant stripped the garden bare.
"Oh, Anxious Ant, if you take all the
seeds for yourself, where will the new
plants come from next spring?"

Anxious Ant replied, "I don't have time to worry about springtime plants — the winter is coming! I must collect more seeds for my winter rations."

All this worrying and scurrying made Little Spider feel dizzy.
So the clever Spider hatched a plan.

"Oh, Anxious Ant, can I interest you in a trade? In exchange for just five seeds, I will spin you a scarf of the finest silk to keep you warm through the cold winter. And I'll make you a promise. Next springtime I'll show you how to transform these five seeds into a whole mountain of seeds. It's the most wonderful magic of all — Seed Magic!"

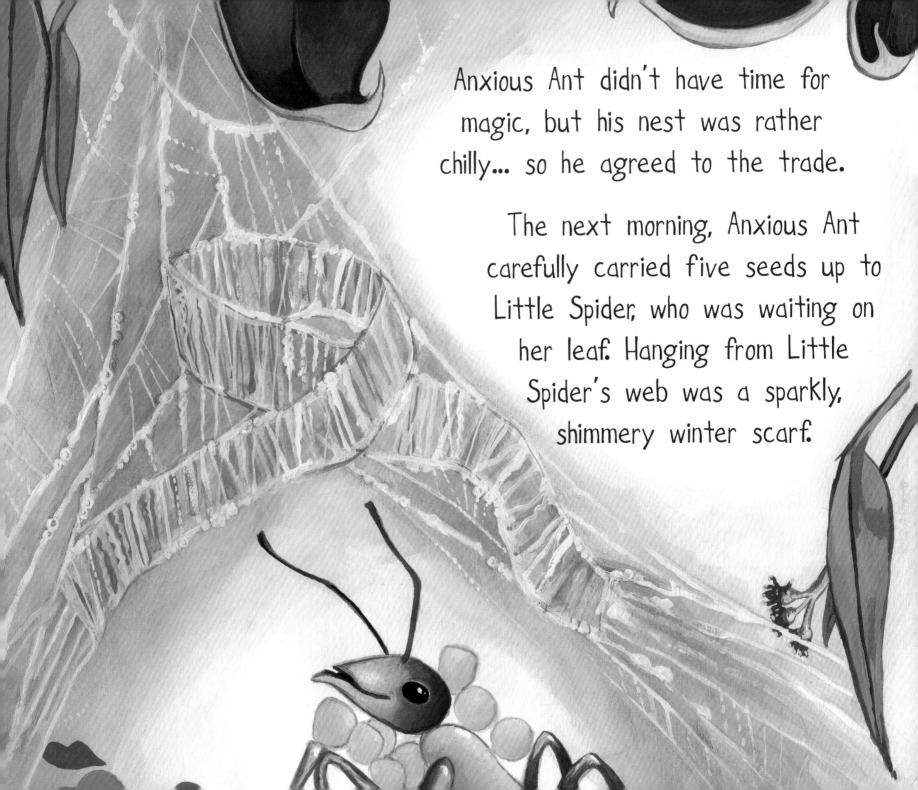

Anxious Ant didn't have time for magic, but his nest was rather chilly... so he agreed to the trade.

The next morning, Anxious Ant carefully carried five seeds up to Little Spider, who was waiting on her leaf. Hanging from Little Spider's web was a sparkly, shimmery winter scarf.

...until each developed juicy fruit.

With the help of the spring
rain and sunshine, the five
tiny seeds sprouted into
delicate seedlings.

Which grew...
and grew...

And then they waited... and waited...

Little Spider showed Anxious Ant how to gently sow each
seed in a warm, sunny spot in the garden.

When the winter frost began to thaw,
Little Spider called to Anxious Ant, "Wake
up, Ant — it's time to see some Seed
Magic! Come watch me turn these five
seeds into a whole pile of seeds!"

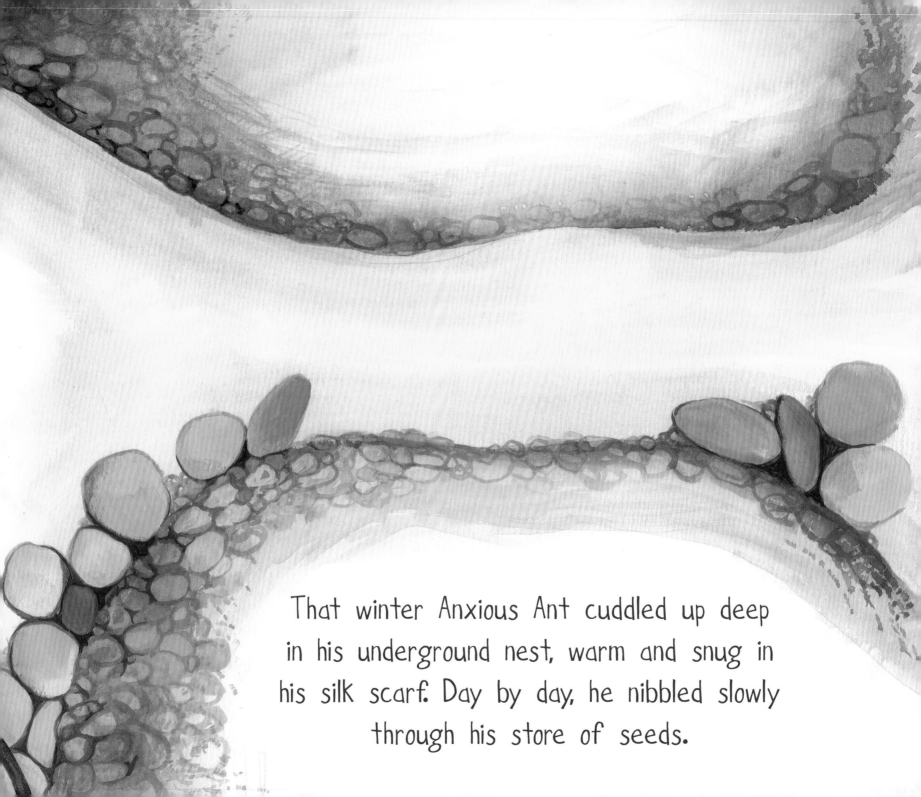

That winter Anxious Ant cuddled up deep in his underground nest, warm and snug in his silk scarf. Day by day, he nibbled slowly through his store of seeds.

Little Spider and Anxious Ant waited...
and waited...

In the summertime, some of the fruit
fell to the ground, making a delicious
feast for the two friends.

Little Spider and Anxious Ant waited...
and waited...

...until the remaining fruit shriveled and dried up in the hot summer sun.
When the autumn winds began to blow once more, the wrinkly fruit tumbled to the ground.
"Woosh!"
The fruit burst open and out scattered hundreds of seeds!

"That's amazing!" exclaimed Anxious Ant.

"I never knew that five little seeds could become so many more like these! You've changed my life — I'll never be anxious for the Winter again."

And no more did Little Spider hear:
Hurry, scurry, worry-worry,
Hurry, scurry, worry-worry...

...because now Anxious Ant knew that if he
carefully saved a few Autumn seeds to plant
in the Spring, he could turn them into a whole
pile of seeds for next year. He had learned
Seed Magic!

An Imprint of Starfish Bay Publishing
www.starfishbaypublishing.com
STARFISH BAY is a trademark of Starfish Bay Publishing Pty Ltd.

SEED MAGIC

Text copyright © Natalie McKinnon, 2018
Illustrations copyright © Margaret Tolland, 2018
Printed and bound in China by Beijing Shangtang Print & Packaging Co., Ltd.
11 Tengren Road, Niulanshan Town, Shunyi District, Beijing, China
ISBN 978-1-76036-031-3

Sincere thanks to Jenny Crowhurst and Elyse Williams from Starfish Bay Children's Books for their creative efforts in preparing this edition for publication.

Natalie McKinnon is an early childhood educator with over 20 years' teaching experience in Australia. Natalie also presents environmental workshops for preschool and elementary audiences. Her workshops encourage children to understand where real food comes from and to develop an understanding of the relationship between their health and the environment.

Margaret Tolland is a New Zealand artist and teacher. Margaret's work is centred on themes of conservation, with detailed illustrations exploring the habitats and lifestyles of many species of flora and fauna. With a 20-year career in arts education, Margaret currently works as an educator at Pataka Museum. In 2014, she was a finalist in the New Zealand Post Book Awards for Children and Young Adults.